The Little Warriors
Be Brave Ranch

THE GRAVEYARD
And Other Not-So-Scary Stories

Weekly Reader Books presents

THE GRAVEYARD

And Other Not-So-Scary Stories

by William E. Warren

illustrated by Edward Frascino

cover illustration by Dick Maccabe

Prentice-Hall, Inc.
Englewood Cliffs, New Jersey

This book is a presentation of Weekly Reader Books.
Weekly Reader Books offers book clubs for children from
preschool through high school.

For further information write to:
Weekly Reader Books
4343 Equity Drive
Columbus, Ohio 43228

Printed in the United States of America   ·J

Prentice-Hall International, Inc., London
Prentice-Hall of Australia, Pty. Ltd., Sydney
Prentice-Hall Canada, Inc., Toronto
Prentice-Hall of India Private Ltd., New Delhi
Prentice-Hall of Japan, Inc., Tokyo
Prentice-Hall of Southeast Asia Pte. Ltd., Singapore
Whitehall Books Limited, Wellington, New Zealand
Editora Prentice-Hall do Brasil LTDA., Rio de Janeiro

10 9 8 7 6 5 4 3 2 1

Library of Congress Cataloging in Publication Data

Warren, William E.
  The graveyard and other not so scary stories.

  Summary: Short stories, each presented in a split
sequence: the first leaves the reader on the verge of
horror; the second presents an ordinary explanation for
the situation.
    1. Children's stories, American. 2. Horror tales,
American. [1. Horror stories. 2. Humorous stories.
3. Short stories] I. Frascino, Edward, ill. II. Title.
PZ7.W2572Gr 1984   [Fic.] -   83-23125
ISBN 0-13-363623-2

For
Wendi, Jenny, Kristen, and Nickie

WARNING!!!

The four stories contained in this book do not progress in normal order. For reasons that will become obvious as you read, each story has been divided into sections that are separated from each other by parts from the other stories.

Do not read the book straight through from cover to cover. Instead, follow the directions at the end of each section of the story you're reading.

To begin, turn to the next page and select the story you want to read.

CONTENTS

THE GRAVEYARD

The rusty hinges scream in protest as you push your way through the gate and enter the old cemetery. Behind you are your best friends Terry and Lisa—and your little brother Mitchie. He's only six years old and harder to get rid of than a wart.

"I don't think I like this. It's scary in here," you complain.

The moon is full tonight. In its glow, the gravestones look like animals crouched and ready to pounce on you.

"Hey, you're crazy!" Terry says, laughing. "This is the most popular place in town. People are dying to get in here!"

You and Lisa look at each other and groan. Terry knows more corny jokes than anybody.

"His father is a mortician," Lisa says.

"A mortician? What's that?" Mitchie asks.

"He buries people," you reply.

"Only the dead ones," Terry says with a laugh. "We have a great layaway plan. You stab 'em, we slab 'em. And if they're not a phantom, we plant 'em."

The moon disappears behind a cloud briefly, then reappears.

"How many dead people are in here?" Mitchie asks.

"All of 'em," Terry replies. His laughter is loud enough to wake the dead. You hope it won't, though.

"You're a million laughs, Terry," Lisa says.

"Like father, like son," you add.

"Hey, don't knock my dad," Terry says. "You can count on Dad; he's the last person in the world who'll ever let you down!"

Even Mitchie groans this time.

"I still don't think we should be here." You glance around nervously.

Lisa frowns. "You can always turn around and go back home if you want to."

You glare at her. "I can take it if you can."

Suddenly, a shiver passes through you, although it's not cold outside. You've just had the strangest feeling: *Someone in your group is in dreadful danger!*

Is it Mitchie?

No such luck, you decide. Monsters don't eat other monsters, not even little ones like Mitchie.

You glance toward Terry. No, he's so lucky that he could walk through quicksand without getting wet.

What about Lisa, then? As you shift your gaze toward her, your heart pounds in sudden fear. Something large is moving toward her in the damp grass! It pauses, gathering itself to spring at her.

"Lisa, look out!" you shout. But it's too late. Lisa screams, and her face twists in horror as she is attacked from behind by an enormous

(Turn to page 12)

ALL ALONE

The sounds!

You never knew so many of them existed before. Creaking sounds from inside the walls, as if the house itself were groaning under its own weight. The wind moaning through the attic vents, the air conditioner clicking on and off—a thousand other tiny noises you'll never identify. The sounds of an old house growing older.

Or dying.

It's scary being alone at night. Mom and Dad left hours ago to play bridge with friends, leaving you to babysit with your younger brother Mitchie. He's asleep now in his bedroom down the hall.

You glance at the old grandfather clock next to the door. It's twelve-thirty. Mom and Dad won't like it when they come home and find you up, but you couldn't sleep now if you tried.

On the eleven o'clock news you heard that a prison escapee has been seen in the area. The news report stated that the man is a convicted murderer. He is listed as armed and dangerous.

So you're trying to watch television. But you jump in your seat and jerk your head around whenever you hear a noise. Each time, you're relieved to find no one standing behind you, reaching for you.

Suddenly, a blood-curdling scream jolts you out of your seat again. It's Mitchie! Something's wrong with Mitchie!

You leap to your feet and dash down the hall. As you arrive, the doorknob to his room begins to turn.

"Mitchie?"

There's no answer. Nothing but the doorknob twisting and the door to Mitchie's room opening ever so slowly. Then Mitchie steps into view. The front of his pajamas is soaked in blood. You stare at him in stunned silence.

"Help me," Mitchie says weakly. "I've been

(Turn to page 16)

THE HAUNTED HOUSE

"This is it."

The cab driver steers his taxi over to the curb. He stares uneasily at the dark two-story mansion to your left. "Boy, I wouldn't want to be in your shoes!"

"Why not?" your younger brother Mitchie asks as you pay the driver.

"Are you kidding?" the cabbie replies. "Look at that place! It looks like something you'd see in one of those old monster movies!"

He's right, too. The old house, barely visible in the foggy evening, is badly in need of repairs. What little paint you can see on it is flaky and gray with age. You find it hard to believe that anyone could be living there.

"I think it's neat," Mitchie says. But of course he'd say that. He's six years old, and everybody knows that six-year-olds are crazy. Mitchie would like it even if there were a dozen werewolves waiting for you on the front porch.

"Are you sure this is the right address?" you ask the cabbie uneasily.

"Yep," he replies. "This is Transylvania Avenue, and the

7

number above the door says six sixty-six. Who did you say you were going to see?"

"Uncle Frank!" Mitchie shouts before you can reply.

"That's it, then," the cabbie says. He points to the name DR. FRANKLIN N. STYNE neatly lettered on a rusty old mailbox.

When the taxi finally leaves, you look at the dark sky and wonder what time it is. Both of Mickey Mouse's hands are missing from your wristwatch, but someone else's hands are firmly planted around Mickey's throat.

"Well, let's go," you say. The house looms over you like a hungry monster. "You go first, Mitchie."

Mitchie runs on ahead of you in the fog, leaving you to carry the bags along the narrow tree-lined sidewalk.

With every step you take, you expect to meet a blood-crazed beast or a snarling monster reaching for your throat from out of the fog with twisted, clawlike fingers.

Then, just as you decide that the terrible night sounds around you are just your imagination, you hear a scream somewhere ahead of you in the fog.

"Mitchie!" You rush through the fog and up the steps onto the front porch.

Mitchie is standing by the front door. His eyes are wide, his mouth gaping open as he stares down at his feet.

"Mitchie, are you all right?"

"Yeah, but look." Mitchie points toward the object at his feet.

"Oh, no," you gasp, staring at it. "It can't be!"

But it is. Lying on the floor at your brother's feet is the twisted remains of a dead

(Turn to page 13)

SPIDERS AND SNAKES

You're lying in bed. You're supposed to be asleep, but you can't sleep for thinking about what's in store for you.

Your father, who's in charge of the Reptile House at the zoo, wants you to help him tomorrow. You've been to the zoo many times before, but Dad wouldn't let you work with him. He thought you were too young.

When you argued with him about it, he explained that it's not dangerous work as long as you concentrate on what you're doing and don't make mistakes. But he was afraid that you'd try to handle the reptiles, or maybe leave a cage open when you were feeding them.

Apparently he's changed his mind, though. Dad told you this evening that, if you'd promise to be careful, you could work with him at the Reptile House for a few days.

Of course, you quickly agreed not to take any chances. But as you lie in bed, you see yourself kneeling in front of an enormous king cobra that has escaped from its cage. Behind you, frozen in their tracks as if hypnotized by the snake, a group of

9

spectators watch in horrified fascination as you wave one hand slowly up and down to attract the cobra's attention.

Then, as the cobra hisses loudly, spreads its hood, and turns its head slightly toward your hand, your other hand darts out and grasps the huge snake by its hooded neck. The spectators applaud as you carry the squirming cobra back to its cage before it can harm anyone.

The vision shifts. In your mind, you see yourself leaping over the protective railing and into the shallow water of the alligator pit to rescue a small child that has fallen into the pit. All around the child, alligators and small crocodiles snap at each other in their eagerness to be the first to reach their victim.

As you land in the knee-deep water, one particularly large creature, a Nile crocodile that is twenty feet long and weighs more than 1,500 pounds, has driven the others away and is preparing to attack.

"Run!" you call to the crying child, splashing the water loudly to attract the crocodile's attention.

Your strategy works! As the huge beast swings its head around violently to face you, the child crawls out of the shallow pool and onto the bank where spectators quickly lift him to safety.

You turn to rush out of the pool, but your feet slip and down you go into the murky water. Even before your head clears the surface, you know that there's no time for you to get out. The charging crocodile will have you in the deadly grasp of its hideous jaws in less than a second.

Suddenly

(Turn to page 15)

grasshopper. It's the biggest grasshopper you've ever seen.

Lisa brushes the insect off her leg. Now it's *her* turn to shiver.

"In Japan, they fry 'em and eat 'em," Terry says.

He picks up the grasshopper and studies it closely. For an awful moment, you think he's going to eat it, the way he is holding it up to his face. But then he tosses it away.

"Ugh!" Lisa says.

The moon disappears behind a cloud. "You know," Terry says in an eerie, whispery voice, "this would be a great night for werewolves!"

Then the moon reappears. You gasp as huge, ghostly spirits seem to rise out of the graves and hover a foot or two above the ground.

As if on signal, the shapeless spirits sweep toward the four of you. You glance at your two friends and Mitchie, but they don't seem to notice. You want to shout and warn them, but you're speechless with fear.

Your eyes bulge in terror as you feel silky fingers touching you gently. You try to call out, but it's too late, even if you could. Already, the four of you are in the grips of

(Turn to page 17)

battery.

"It's a dead battery," you mutter.

"I know," Mitchie says. "I stubbed my toe on it. I wonder what it's doing here."

"I don't know," you reply, "but if it's dead, this looks like the perfect place for it."

Suddenly, the front door opens. A huge creature fills the doorway, then steps swiftly toward Mitchie with arms extended. Each hand is as large as a boxing glove.

"Uncle Frank!" Mitchie cries, rushing to embrace Dr. Styne.

"I'm so glad to see you," your uncle says as he shakes your hand. "I'm glad you could come for a visit. I always look forward to seeing blood kin. You're just what this stuffy old place needs: *new blood*."

He smiles as he ushers you and Mitchie into the house.

His smile, you decide, is as fake as your teacher's pearl necklace. It's as if you and Mitchie are pieces of fried chicken and Uncle Frank can't decide which one to eat first.

"I suppose I should begin by telling you my secret," Uncle Frank says. He closes the heavy front door with a slam and locks it from the inside with a key. Pocketing the key, he turns and draws himself up to his full height, which is considerable.

"You were going to find out sooner or later," he continues, "so I may as well get it over with. You see . . ."

He pauses to lick his lips as he glances from Mitchie to you. "I'm a vampire

(Turn to page 19)

the daydream is over and you're back in your bedroom, wide awake.

Maybe it's because you've been perspiring so heavily, but you realize now that you're thirsty. You sit up and slide your feet over the edge of the bed, intending to go to the kitchen for a drink of water. Your feet never reach the floor, though.

Instead, your foot hits something that twists away and rattles angrily as you put more of your weight on it. You lean over the edge of the bed, expecting the worst. Sure enough, lying coiled at your feet is a long, thick

(Turn to page 21)

eating jelly sandwiches in bed again, and I guess I went to sleep." Mitchie's voice trails off into a series of sobs.

You stare at him. He's covered from his face to his knees with raspberry jelly.

"Mom's not gonna like this," you say as you lead Mitchie toward the bathroom.

"I know," Mitchie says between sobs.

Finally, he's cleaned up and back in bed. You calm him down. As he drifts off to sleep, you tiptoe out of his room and close the door gently behind you.

Your next task is to clean up the kitchen. You know it must be a mess, since Mitchie isn't exactly neat, even for a six-year-old.

When you turn on the kitchen light, you can't believe the scene before your eyes. Judging by the mess, Mitchie must have lined up pieces of bread on the kitchen table and then thrown handfuls of jelly at them from across the room.

You clean up as well as you can, then wash the knife Mitchie used to spread the jelly. While putting the utensils back in their drawer, you notice that the largest knife in your mom's carving set is missing.

Suddenly, the room doesn't seem so friendly anymore.

You turn to put the jelly in the refrigerator. You look up and gasp to find the huge knife poised above your head, less than a foot from your eyes. As the blade begins its downward plunge, you realize dimly that the escaped convict must have broken into

(Turn to page 20)

the thickest fog you've ever seen.

"Hey, this is perfect!" Terry says. "Fog is nice, isn't it?"

"Yeah, sure," you reply. "All we need now is an axe murderer."

"Why would anybody want to murder an axe?" Mitchie asks innocently.

Terry laughs and throws an arm around your brother's shoulder. "You know, kid, you're not so bad for a little wimp—"

"Listen!" Lisa interrupts. Terry pauses, and the four of you listen intently to the night sounds around you.

At first, all you can hear are frogs and toads croaking off-key and crickets sawing tunes on their violin-legs. But then you hear it, the unmistakable sound of footsteps moving slowly toward your little group.

"Are any of you doing that?" Lisa asks in a quivering voice.

You, Terry, and Mitchie look at each other and shake your heads no.

"That's what I thought!" Lisa says. She sprints away in the fog without another word. You and Terry race after her, leaving Mitchie behind.

Let the little creep save himself, you think. You're ashamed of yourself, but you're too frightened to stop and wait for him to catch up with you.

"Wait!" you hear Mitchie calling from somewhere behind you. You can't stop, though: it's everyone for himself now!

You glance behind you as you run, hoping to see Mitchie catching up with you. But he's too little to run that fast.

Ahead of you, waiting silently in the mist, the creature stands with its arms extended to receive you. And as you look backward to find Mitchie, you run directly into its grasp.

The impact of your collision slams you to the ground and

leaves you gasping for breath. You look up slowly to find the great beast towering above you, a monstrous dark shadow that could only be

(Turn to page 23)

bat collector. I collect vampire bats."

"I collect stamps," you mutter weakly.

Later, after an early supper, you and Mitchie are in your bedroom on the second floor. You decide to go downstairs for a snack from the refrigerator. Mitchie appears to be sound asleep as you tiptoe out of your room and close the door softly behind you.

You move silently along the dark hallway and pass downstairs along a broad, curving stairway. At the bottom of the stairs is a suit of armor. You tiptoe past it into the kitchen and try the light switch.

Nothing happens.

Oh well, you decide, you'll still be able to see by the light from the refrigerator. But ever since you arrived at your uncle's house, you've had the feeling that something is terribly wrong. You wonder why you feel that way.

You open the refrigerator slowly. As the light blinks on, you find yourself facing a hideous, grinning skull

(Turn to page 25)

someone else's house. Apparently, your idiot brother tried to put the bread knife on top of the refrigerator. But because he's so small, he couldn't push it back far enough. When you opened the refrigerator door, it began to fall.

You leap backward and easily avoid the plunging knife.

Mom would love to hear about this, you decide as you replace the knife in the cabinet drawer. You turn off the overhead light and walk out of the kitchen into the dark hallway.

As you pass the open doorway to your parents' bedroom, a slight movement among the shadows catches your eye. Even as you realize that the dark shape is human, the shadowy figure leaps

(Turn to page 29)

section of rope that your younger brother Mitchie was playing with earlier. Tangled up with the rope is an overturned can that contained Mitchie's marbles.

After arriving at the zoo with your father the next morning, you wander around the Reptile House while he tends to reports and other matters. You move slowly from cage to cage, staring in fascination at your favorite snakes, the ones you look at every time you come to the zoo:

The deadly Gaboon viper, a heavy-browed brown-and-black snake that always looks like it's frowning. Its fangs (though you can't see them) are nearly two inches long.

The large nervous Eastern diamondback rattlesnake, with its rattles drumming like playing cards being shuffled.

The heavy 18-foot anaconda from South America, lying in a shallow pool in its cage with only its snout exposed to air.

And most fascinating of all, the slender gray 15-foot king cobra, whose venom is so powerful that one drop can kill 150 people or more. You'd like the king to lift itself up into its hooded stance, but it won't. You're tempted to tap on the glass, but if Dad caught you doing that, he'd never let you come with him again.

The indigo snake is your favorite, though. Dad has let you handle it before; it's more harmless than your dog Ralph. It's a shiny, inky black color and feels dry to the touch, not slimy or slippery.

There are other animals in the Reptile House, of course— spiders and scorpions and gila monsters and salamanders and frogs and toads and turtles. You watch them all in turn. You wish you could work here all the time.

Then Dad returns from his office and motions for you to follow him.

"I want to show you something," he says. You follow him, as he unlocks a door and takes you back to an area closed to the public.

"Look," he says, pointing.

In front of you is a small pool that looks like a miniature version of the alligator pool outside. In the pool are ten or twelve little yellow-and-black striped animals that look like fat lizards.

"They're baby alligators, only three days old," Dad says. He walks over and picks up one of them and brings it to you. It makes little sounds in its throat that sound like it hasn't digested its dinner.

"Do you want to hold it?" Dad asks.

(Turn to page 48)

an old oak tree. Its limbs tower over you like gnarled, twisted arms in the misty moonlight.

"Mitchie, where are you?" you whisper urgently as you climb to your feet.

"I'm over here," a frightened, high-pitched voice replies. You hear footsteps advancing in your direction. In a matter of seconds Mitchie appears from out of the fog. You can see that he's been crying.

"I'm gonna tell," Mitchie warns, frowning despite his tears. "You left me, and I'm gonna tell Mom."

"If you do, she'll know that you sneaked out at night when you were supposed to be in bed asleep."

"I don't care," Mitchie says stubbornly. "I'll tell Mom that you kidnapped me. I'll say that—"

"Hush!" you whisper, listening. "Did you hear that?"

The two of you pause, still as death.

"What is it?" Mitchie asks. You motion for him to be quiet.

But now you don't hear anything unusual, just the ordinary, terrifying sounds you always hear in a graveyard at night.

"It sounded like somebody breathing," you say finally, in a voice just above a whisper.

"Maybe it was the wind," Mitchie suggests. You frown at him and shake your head. There hasn't been any wind this evening.

"Well, maybe it was Terry and Lisa," Mitchie says.

"Yeah, maybe that's who it was." But you don't really believe it. Didn't Lisa hear footsteps earlier when the four of you were together?

"I think we ought to go home," Mitchie says.

You nod in agreement. The two of you turn back toward the entrance and find yourselves facing a twisted, shadowy figure ten feet away. You can't see who it is, but it's much too large to be Terry or Lisa. The figure is breathing heavily and dragging one leg slightly as it shuffles toward you in the fog.

You turn to run, only to trip over a large exposed root of the oak tree. Tears come to your eyes as your nose crashes painfully into the ground.

Before you can regain your feet, a cold hand clamps down on your shoulder. You hear deep, rasping breathing above and behind you.

"Run, Mitchie!" you shout. You turn over slowly and find yourself looking up into a large, hairy face.

You stare at the cruel face in mounting terror. You can feel its hot breath as it leans toward you. Its twisted grin reveals a set of

(Turn to page 26)

and crossbones on a wall poster beside the refrigerator. Beneath the skull and crossbones is the caption: *Cigarette Smoking May Be Hazardous To Your Health.*

You reach for a glass from the sink and fill it to the brim with cold milk. Setting the glass aside momentarily, you reach for a pack of sliced ham on the top shelf of the refrigerator.

Suddenly, from out of the darkness, a hand drops onto your shoulder.

You gasp and turn your head, only to find that it's not a hand, but white, meatless fingers that are gripping you.

You whirl around and find yourself staring into the hollow, lifeless eyes of

(Turn to page 30)

empty gums that are badly in need of a set of false teeth.

"What are you kids doing here?" the old man asks.

"We—we were just on our way home from a movie," you reply, thinking fast.

"Little bit late for a show, isn't it?"

"It was a late show." You rise to your feet and dust yourself off.

The old man hovers over you like a buzzard circling overhead. You wish he'd back up a few feet; his breath smells like rotten cabbage.

"I know what you're thinking," the old man says, eyeing you suspiciously.

"You do?"

"Yeah. You're thinking that because I'm an old man with arthritis and emphysema, you can run away from me." He pronounces the words *arthur-itis* and *emfa-zeema*.

"Well, let me tell you one thing," he continues. "You're not going anywhere. My dog Bo is around here someplace. And if I tell him to, Bo will rip you into little bitty pieces before you can move a muscle. He's a trained killer, old Bo is! He'll tear you limb from limb. All I have to do is tell him to."

"I won't run away," you say. Before the caretaker can reply, you're sprinting off into the fog.

You have no idea which direction you're heading, but it doesn't matter. Anywhere is fine, as long as it's far away from the toothless old man and his cabbage breath.

Behind you, the old caretaker's croaking voice cuts through the fog like a knife. "Bo! Kill!"

Soon, over the pounding of your feet on the wet, dewy ground and the urgent throbbing of your heartbeat in your ears, you hear a new and terrifying sound: a low growling somewhere behind you. It is growing louder with every passing second.

The caretaker has released his dog after you, with orders to kill.

"Terry! Lisa!" you shout in mindless fear as you race blindly through the fog.

"Over here!" Terry's voice calls from somewhere to your left. You alter your course, wondering how long it will be before the dog springs and drags you down onto the soggy ground.

After that, the struggle will be brief: if you try to protect your face, the dog will go for your throat.

And if you drop your hands to protect your throat . . .

The dog is narrowing the distance between you. Already you can hear its feverish panting. You know that if you turn around, you'll be able to see the wildness in its eyes and saliva dripping from its jaws.

Suddenly, as you pass the entrance to the cemetery's mausoleum, a hand snakes out and jerks you inside.

The door slams shut.

Outside, the watchman's dog is pawing frantically at the door, trying to reach you.

Inside the room, you turn to face the numbing terror of

(Turn to page 32)

too, because it's your own reflection in your mom's mirror.

A sudden crash of thunder and lightning outside makes the lights flicker off and on. You decide that you'd better have candles ready in case the electricity goes off.

With a shrug of your shoulders and a final glance at the dark reflection of yourself in the mirror, you turn away from your parents' bedroom. Then, as an afterthought, you turn back and close the door.

The candles, you recall, are in a kitchen cabinet. You don't want to go back into the kitchen, but you have no choice.

As you walk down the hall, the rain begins. It drums against the roof and windows like an endless parade of tiny marching soldiers. The wind whistles and moans.

The lights flicker off again, then return, this time more slowly. Somewhere above your head, you hear a scraping sound like something heavy being dragged across the roof. You *know* it's not Santa Claus; you *hope* it's not the escaped convict dragging the body of his latest victim.

The culprit, you decide, is probably a tree limb dragging back and forth against the roof.

You pause outside the kitchen and reach around the door-frame to turn on the light.

The room seems peaceful enough, but a puddle of water has gathered on the floor in front of the sink. The curtains are whipping back and forth from the driving wind and rain.

You rush to the sink and close and lock the window. Not until you return from the pantry with a mop do you notice the wet, dirty footprint in the middle of the floor.

A frown crosses your face as you study the print. At the same time, a movement to your right catches your attention. As you look up he springs, crashing into your chest and driving you backward onto the hardwood floor.

(Turn to page 42)

Jarvis, your uncle's butler.

Jarvis drops his hand from your shoulder.

He isn't tall, but he stands so stiffly erect that he looks like he's about to tip over backward. His eyes, deep-set and piercing, are two X-ray machines that could read a newspaper held behind your head. You just know that if he smiled at you, you'd see a pair of long, dripping fangs curling out of the corners of his mouth.

"You scared me to *death*!" you say.

"Sorry," Jarvis says in a deep, lifeless voice. "I thought you might be a prowler. Guests normally turn the lights on."

"I tried them, but they didn't work."

"Indeed." Jarvis walks over to the wall and raises a white gloved hand to flip the light switch on. The room fills with light instantly.

"Well, they wouldn't come on earlier," you say as you sit down at the kitchen table.

"I'm sure you're right." The butler's tone implies that he doesn't believe a word you've said. "Will there be anything else?"

Your mouth is too full of ham to reply, so you shake your head no.

"I believe I'll retire for the night then, if you don't mind."

Without waiting for a reply, Jarvis turns and walks out of the room as silently as a ghost. Seconds after he leaves, the lights in the room blink off again, leaving you in almost total darkness.

You feel around the table until you locate your glass of milk. You manage to empty its contents in three or four swallows. Then, having finished off the ham, you pick up the empty glass.

As you feel your way in the dark toward the sink, a horrible thought enters your mind.

What if when you reach down to place the glass in the sink, a slimy, dripping hand reaches up through the drain opening and closes on your wrist?

And what if the cold rotting hand grips you in a death lock and begins to pull you down toward the place under the sink that it calls home?

By the time you reach the counter, you're so completely overcome with fear that you'd like to toss the glass into the sink and dart out of the room.

You won't do that, though. The glass would shatter and wake up everyone in the house. So you slide ever so slowly toward the edge of the sink, hoping that when you look down, you won't see fingers creeping up through the dark opening and feeling around, searching for you.

Through the window above the sink, you can see the full moon coming out from behind the clouds. Moonlight streams into the room, outlining objects and permitting you to see.

Holding your breath, you peer down into the sink.

You drop the glass. Only dimly do you hear the crash as it bursts into thousands of tiny pieces on the floor. You stand as if paralyzed, gazing at the only object in the sink: a hand

(Turn to page 35)

a room enveloped in total darkness.

Despite your relief at escaping the night watchman's dog, you are still uneasy. After all, someone (or something) dragged you into the mausoleum.

What if it wasn't Terry or Lisa?

What if, instead of your friends, you're trapped inside the house of tombs with a creature that isn't quite dead?

And what if the next sound you hear is the unearthly laughter of something from beyond the grave, giggling because at last it has found a playmate to take back with it?

"That was close," Terry says. Relief floods over you.

"Is Lisa here too?" you ask weakly.

"I'm here," Lisa whispers.

"Where's Mitchie?" you ask. "Haven't you seen him?"

"We thought he was with you," Lisa replies.

"He was, but—well, it's a long story. The important thing is that Mitchie's out there and we're in here!" You shudder at the thought of being inside the creepy mausoleum at night.

"And the caretaker's dog is out there, too," Terry says.

"You—you *knew* he had a ferocious dog and you still brought us here?" Lisa asks. "Honestly, Terry, sometimes I think you must take stupid pills!"

You resist the temptation to point out to Lisa that you didn't want to come here in the first place. There are other, more important things to think about now.

"We've got to get out of here and help Mitchie," you say.

"Maybe the dog is gone by now," Terry says. He opens the door and sticks his head out. Then he ducks back inside and slams the door shut just as the snarling dog crashes into the door.

"So much for that idea," Lisa says. "Is there a back door to this place?"

"No," Terry answers. "This is the only entrance or exit."

"Wait!" you say urgently. "I think I heard something! It sounded like a voice."

"I hope it was *outside*," Lisa says. Her meaning is obvious, but you shush her anyway.

Then you hear it again: Mitchie's voice, calling you as if from far away. You open the door slowly and poke your head out, expecting another attack. But the dog, a vicious doberman, is gone.

And you know where he's gone.

After Mitchie. Your little brother won't stand a chance.

You fling the door wide open and hurry outside.

"Mitchie, run! Get out of here!" you shout.

"I can't!" Mitchie's voice drifts back to you through the fog.

"We've got to help him!" Lisa says. "But how? We haven't anything we can use as a weapon."

"There's a rake over here," Terry says.

"Let's go, then!" you say. The three of you rush off in the direction Mitchie's voice came from.

"Mitchie, we're coming!" you cry as you run. You listen for a reply, but there is none. The silence is like a dagger twisting in your heart.

You're going to be too late. You wish you'd told Mitchie to climb a tree to get away from the dog. But everything happened so fast that you weren't able to think clearly.

In your mind's eye, you envision the scene as you reach Mitchie. He's lying on the ground with the caretaker's dog standing over him. As you approach, the dog turns to face you. Blood is dripping from its jaws.

Suddenly, the fog parts and you *can* see Mitchie. He's lying on the ground ahead of you and to your left.

The doberman is standing over him, just as it was in your

vision. The dog towers above Mitchie like an executioner at the chopping block.

As you slow your approach to a walk, the dog growls menacingly, baring its fangs.

"You'd better get in front with the rake, Terry," Lisa says. But Terry has vanished, swallowed up by the thick fog.

"That's great," you say. "We've got to help Mitchie. But what do we do if the dog decides to attack?"

Then, as if reading your mind, the doberman steps forward.

(Turn to page 36)

carved mahogany salad bowl that Jarvis must have overlooked when he washed the supper dishes.

The overhead light blinks on. You look up, expecting to find Jarvis or Uncle Frank standing in the doorway.

No one's there, though.

You kneel to pick up the pieces of glass on the floor, and that's when you hear the sound of voices talking low.

At first you think it's Jarvis and Uncle Frank coming to investigate the noise you made. But then, as the voices continue and no one enters the kitchen, you realize that the voices are coming from behind a door to the left of the hallway.

You rise, tiptoe over to the door, and open it as quietly as possible. It leads, you find, to a cellar. You can't see clearly from your present location, so you pause to listen to the conversation downstairs.

"—have to kill him tonight," a deep voice is saying. It sounds like Jarvis, the butler, but you can't be sure.

"If we fail tonight," the voice continues, "we'll be discovered tomorrow, and all will be lost."

A voice speaking so softly that you can't hear it plainly says something, and the Jarvis-voice answers, "I think a stake through the heart would do nicely, sir."

You realize with a start that he's talking about *you*. Your mind tells you to rush upstairs, wake Mitchie, and get away from the house before Jarvis can finish his evil task.

Unfortunately, your feet aren't listening to your mind.

Instead of sneaking away, you find yourself moving silently onto the landing at the top of the stairs and closing the door behind you. Then you tiptoe down four steps to find out who is talking about killing you.

(Turn to page 39)

"Bo!" Mitchie calls out sharply. The dog halts immediately and steps back to stand by Mitchie's side. Mitchie pats the doberman affectionately.

"Good boy," he says quietly.

"Mitchie, are you all right?" you ask.

"Sure! Me and Bo are friends. You two want to pet him?"

Lisa glances at you. "No, thanks. Go ahead if you want to. I'll wait over here."

You turn back to Mitchie. "Can you control Bo while we walk out of here?"

"Sure. Why not?" Mitchie rises and addresses the dog. "Now, Bo, you be nice and I'll bring you a cookie tomorrow."

The dog wags its tail and licks Mitchie's hand.

"How do we get out of here?" you ask Lisa.

She points behind her. "I think the exit is back that way."

The three of you walk off into the fog, with the caretaker's vicious watchdog trotting happily beside Mitchie like a puppy.

Suddenly, the doberman halts and growls menacingly.

"Uh-oh," Lisa says as the three of you halt in mid-step.

"What is it?" you ask.

"I don't know," Lisa replies, "but if the dog doesn't like it, I don't think I do either."

You glance around nervously as Bo continues to growl. You hear a faint scraping sound that you can't locate in the fog and the darkness. You walk forward slowly, listening.

All around you are tombs and gravestones. As the moon slides out from behind a cloud, you notice a dark opening in the grass a few feet ahead of you.

It's an open grave.

If it hadn't been for the moonlight, you might have stumbled into the dark pit. And who knows what might have been waiting for you down there?

An image fills your mind: you're picking yourself up from the bottom of the rectangular hole. You brush yourself off and glance upward to see the moon disappearing behind clouds, shutting off the light—

But it isn't the moon disappearing. It's a thick slab of concrete sliding into the place above your head! As the outside world narrows and disappears, you hear Lisa and Mitchie calling your name frantically.

And then there's nothing but silence, and the blackest darkness imaginable.

You're trapped. Forever.

Your screams for help go unheard in the darkness of your ghostly prison. Finally, you realize that your screaming is wasting your precious oxygen supply, so you quit.

Maybe you can dig your way out, though. You begin to claw at the side of the grave near the top, when a bony hand grips your shoulder.

"I've been waiting for you," a deep voice says softly.

(Turn to page 40)

You were right. Jarvis is standing in the middle of the large cellar, clutching a hammer in one hand. Uncle Frank is seated on a sofa, laughing insanely. The echoes of his wild laughter ring to every corner of the room.

Jarvis begins to laugh, too. Soon the two men are howling in fiendish pleasure at the thought of your unfortunate death.

Then, for no apparent reason, the stair beneath your feet squeaks loudly. Uncle Frank and Jarvis jerk their heads around and spot you on the stairway. Jarvis glances at Uncle Frank for instructions.

"Hello," Uncle Frank says. "I didn't know you were still up." His voice is friendly enough, but that doesn't fool you. It's the man with the hammer who is likely to be unfriendly.

"Come on down," your uncle urges. He turns to the butler. "Jarvis, help our young visitor down the stairs."

"That's okay," you say weakly. "I can make it by myself." You walk downstairs slowly on legs that feel as if they weigh a ton apiece.

Uncle Frank smiles grimly. You wonder if he's planning to feed you to his vampire bats.

"Come, come, don't take all night," Uncle Frank says as you pause at the bottom of the stairs with your hand still on the railing.

Uncle Frank's voice is no longer friendly. He rises from the sofa. He is carrying a dark object in his right hand.

It's some kind of control box. Uncle Frank presses a button on the box, and

(Turn to page 44)

You shake your head from side to side vigorously to rid yourself of such awful thoughts. Behind you, Mitchie and Lisa are waiting expectantly. The doberman continues to growl his warning.

The dark grave looms ahead of you. Although you have absolutely no desire to do so, you find yourself edging closer and closer to the open grave.

You pause near the pit. As you gaze into the yawning darkness below you, you're only vaguely aware of Lisa screaming behind you.

But then you see what she's screaming at: a hand snaking out of the blackness of the grave and wrapping itself tightly around your ankle.

You fall to the ground and claw at the earth around you. Meanwhile, the hand is drawing you closer and closer to the edge of the pit.

(Turn to page 45)

"Get off me, Ralph!" you protest. The dog, a frisky German shepherd puppy, is too busy licking your face to respond. Finally, Ralph pauses to shake himself. Water flies from his brown coat onto the floor.

You climb to your feet. "How did you get in, Ralph?"

You already know the answer, though: he got in through the hinged trapdoor at the bottom of the back door. Before long, Ralph will be too big to fit through the opening.

Your dad says that at the rate Ralph is eating now, when he's full-grown he should weigh around eighteen hundred pounds. Dad doesn't like Ralph very much.

You use a dish towel to dry Ralph and then mop up the water on the floor. At times like this, you envy Mitchie for not having responsibilities. He never has to do any work around the house.

Finally, you're ready to leave the kitchen again. You replace the mop in the pantry, toss the wet dish towel in the sink, lean over to scratch Ralph behind his ear briefly, and then turn off the overhead light and leave the room. Ralph follows at your heel.

Halfway down the hall, a sudden burst of thunder and lightning reminds you that you've forgotten the candles. You return to the kitchen, pick up three candles and holders and a box of matches, and turn off the light for the third time. Ralph isn't with you; he must have gone into the living room.

The storm shows no sign of letting up or passing over, you notice as you reenter the living room. Through the large picture window on the opposite side of the room you can see tall trees bending and swaying with the force of the wind.

Ralph is lying in front of the sofa, asleep.

Suddenly, you realize that something isn't right about the

room. A chill passes through you as you become aware that something—you're not sure what—has changed since you left the living room earlier.

Behind you, a pair of long, slender hands are creeping silently toward

(Turn to page 49)

the color television set switches off.

"I never did like that movie," your uncle says. "That was the only good part of the entire show."

"I agree, sir," Jarvis says.

"Go ahead, Jarvis," Uncle Frank says casually. "You may as well do the job now."

"Very good, sir."

Your eyes widen in terror as Jarvis walks toward you with the hammer clutched tightly in his fist.

Why, you wonder, did you have to come down here? Why couldn't you have gone back to your room? Why did you and Mitchie have to come to visit Uncle Frank in the first place? Didn't Mom and Dad know that he's—well, *strange*?

You can see clearly in your mind Jarvis drawing the hammer up and back, smiling coldly at your helplessness. You want to turn and run, but you can't. You're petrified, rooted to the spot like a bird hypnotized by a snake.

Jarvis continues to advance toward you. Your forehead is dotted with perspiration now, but your mouth is dry as a bone.

The butler pauses in front of you. He flexes his fingers for a better grip on the hammer.

This is it, you think grimly. Goodbye, cruel world! Goodbye, Mom and Dad, who sent me here to have fun. Goodbye, Mitchie, who wasn't really such a wimp of a little brother after all! Goodbye—

(Turn to page 50)

"Let go, you're pulling me in!" you shout.

"Well, help me out, then!" Terry replies.

"What were you doing in there in that hole anyway?" Lisa asks as the three of you pull Terry out of the grave.

"I was following a white rabbit," Terry replies sarcastically. Then, when nobody laughs, he adds, "I fell in just before you showed up."

"Was it scary down there?" Mitchie asks.

"Why don't you hop in and see?" Terry replies. He backs up a step as the doberman growls at him.

"Bo is Mitchie's friend," you explain.

"We've met," Terry says.

"This place is creepy," Lisa says. "How do we get out of here?"

"Over here," Terry says, pointing. "It's not far." The three of you and Bo follow Terry to the gate at the side of the cemetery.

"You've got to stay here, Bo," Mitchie says. He pets the doberman, then hugs it lovingly.

"Do you believe that?" Terry asks, watching Mitchie and the dog. "I think I'd feel safer hugging a rattlesnake!"

"Bo's nice," Mitchie argues. Then he adds, "I'll be back with a cookie for you tomorrow, Bo."

The dog wags its stump of a tail happily.

Outside, you glance around. You're standing at the edge of Dead Man's Road, a dark and lonely road half a mile from your house. It's a scary place, even in the daytime.

Dead Man's Road runs along the edge of the woods. And you have to pass through it to get home.

"I think the fog is getting worse," Lisa says quietly.

"It's the swamp," Terry agrees. "It's always foggy at night along here."

The four of you huddle together like baby chicks as you walk slowly along the narrow unpaved road.

Besides yourselves, the only sounds you hear are frogs and toads grunting, crickets fiddling, and an owl hooting somewhere in the distance.

Terry's voice breaks the silence. "They say a man was murdered around here a few years ago."

"Really?" Mitchie asks. "Tell us about it, Terry."

"It was awful," Terry says in a whispery voice. "They say he was walking along Dead Man's Road one night like we are. It was real foggy then, too. Anyway, he thought he heard something, so he stopped. The sound stopped. He listened for a minute, then took a couple of steps and stopped again."

"What happened then?" Mitchie asks.

"The sound moved and stopped, too. The man asked, 'Who's there?' but all he heard was bubbling, squishy sounds coming from the woods."

"Neat!" Mitchie says.

"And then, when the man reached the deepest part of the fog—it was right about here, I think—he heard it."

"What was it?" Mitchie asks excitedly.

"It was the sound of *footsteps*, pounding toward him in the fog!" Terry says. "The man started backing away slowly. As he was trying to decide whether to run or hide, a dark, hairy shape came flying at him from out of the fog!"

Terry's voice grows quieter. "They never found the man. And they say that whatever attacked him is still here, prowling around the road on foggy nights looking for its next victim."

"That's silly," you hear yourself saying. "If they never found the man, how do they know it happened that way?"

"Because he disappeared," Terry argues. "What more proof do you need—"

"Shut up, you two! Listen!" Lisa whispers.

Instantly alert, everyone stops and strains to hear the night sounds coming out of the fog.

"I don't hear anything," Mitchie says.

You do, though. It's a sound that fills your entire body and soul with terror.

Footsteps. Footsteps of someone—or some*thing*—running toward you in the fog.

(Turn to page 52)

"Sure," you say. "Why not?"

Dad hands you the baby 'gator. It *is* like a lizard, only larger and not as fast. It's only about six inches long, but you can imagine what it will look like ten or twelve years from now. It squirms in your hand.

"Tickle it under its chin," Dad suggests. You glance at him to see if he's kidding, but he's not. You do as he says, and the baby 'gator's mouth pops wide open. The inside of its mouth is the softest pastel orange imaginable.

"Put your finger in its mouth," your father says. Then, seeing the look of surprise on your face, he adds, "Go ahead. It won't hurt you. It doesn't have any teeth yet."

You extend your index finger, and the 'gator clamps down on it. It doesn't hurt, but the baby 'gator's jaws grip your finger tightly enough that you let go of it with your other hand and watch it dangling from your index finger.

"Come back two or three months from now and try that," Dad suggests.

"No, thanks," you reply. By then the 'gator will have a mouthful of teeth and enough strength to inflict painful injury to your finger.

"How do I get him off?" you ask.

Dad reaches over and takes hold of the 'gator's body, then taps it lightly on the end of its snout once. Its jaws open and it drops away from your finger.

You smile broadly. "That was neat."

"I thought you'd like it," Dad says. He replaces the baby alligator in its enclosure, then straightens and turns to you.

"I have some free time now," he says. "Let's go see how Tarrie is doing."

"Great!" you reply.

Tarrie is the Reptile House's resident tarantula.

(Turn to page 53)

midnight on the old grandfather clock.

You've got to get a grip on yourself. Your overactive imagination has you jumping at shadows.

Sure, there's a convict on the loose—but he's probably miles away by now. And sure, it's dark and scary outside—but that's true every night.

The difference is that you don't stay up late every night.

It's scary *inside* the house, too. With all the eerie, unexplained noises that occur at night, you wonder how anyone could ever take a job as a night watchman.

You resist the temptation to turn on every light in the room. Dad probably would dock your allowance for wasting money on electricity.

Instead, you walk over to the picture window and look at the stormy world outside. The front yard is cluttered with limbs and leaves. The trees are thrashing in the wind. A voice is whispering in your ear, "I want to drink your blood."

You whirl around and find

(Turn to page 57)

The butler's voice interrupts your goodbyes.

"Huh?" you ask weakly.

"I said 'Excuse me,'" Jarvis says. He steps past you and begins hammering at some loose nails in the railing.

"We wouldn't want you to hurt yourself on the stairway," Jarvis says.

"Step over here," Uncle Frank says. He places a giant hand on your neck. He could snap your neck with a single twist of his hand if he wanted to.

"I like to come down here to get away from the outside world," your uncle says. "I find it very comforting to watch television ten feet underground, don't you?"

You wouldn't answer *that* question for a million dollars!

"But that isn't what I wanted to show you," Uncle Frank continues. "If you'll follow me, I have something over here I think you'll find interesting."

With his hand on your neck, Uncle Frank could lead you anywhere. He steers you to another part of the large basement.

"I conduct experiments here," Uncle Frank says as he pauses. You stare wide-eyed at the machinery and equipment in front of you. It fills that entire portion of the basement.

"Over here," he says. To your right is a large table. An operating table. Your eyes bulge in shock as you stare at it.

Strapped to the table and partially hidden by a sheet is your brother

(Turn to page 59)

"Somebody's coming!" Lisa cries.

"I'm getting out of here!" Terry shouts.

"Me too," Mitchie says.

By now, all four of you hear the advancing footsteps and the deep growl of something you hope you'll never see face to face.

You turn to run, but it's too late. Already, you see a dark, hairy shape hurtling toward Mitchie from out of the fog.

Mitchie, struck from behind, is pounded to the ground as you watch helplessly. Standing over your brother, the beast turns toward you. Its long, sharp fangs are clearly visible.

(Turn to page 63)

Dad leads you through the narrow passageway behind the cages. It's thrilling to realize that only a few inches away on either side of you are some of the most deadly animals on the face of the earth.

On the other side of the cages, thick glass protects zoo visitors from the deadly reptiles and vice versa. On this side, though, all that protects you from each one is a latch and a tiny lock. And all you'd have to do is unfasten the lock and release the latch and you'd find yourself facing an angry black mamba from Africa, or a tiger snake from Australia whose venom is even more powerful than that of the king cobra.

You wonder what it would be like to face a cottonmouth moccasin coiled and ready to strike. The cottonmouth could strike, inject its deadly load of venom, and return to its coiled position in less than a half-second.

Would you even be able to see it strike? How long would it be before you started to feel the effects of its bite?

"Here we are," Dad says, interrupting your thoughts. He releases the lock and unlatches the hinged door on one of the cages. "Wake up, Tarrie, you have visitors."

Dad reaches into the cage slowly, but with a smoothness and confidence you'd never have thought possible.

If it were me reaching in there, you decide, I'd be shaking so badly that Tarrie would think I was attacking her.

Dad gently lifts Tarrie the tarantula out of her cage and places her gently on the back of his hand. She is, you decide, the most horrible, ugly creature you've ever seen. Except for your little brother Mitchie, that is.

"Aren't tarantulas poisonous?" you ask.

"Yes, but not like a cobra or a rattlesnake," your father replies. "Tarrie's a nice girl, though. She won't bite me as long as I don't upset her by squeezing her. She doesn't like to be squeezed."

You stare at the tarantula in fascination. Her eight legs are long and they curve upward and back down as if she were about to pounce on something. (She isn't, though.) Her legs are covered with long black bristly hairs.

"What do you think of her?" Dad asks as Tarrie begins to tiptoe up his wrist.

"I think she needs to shave her legs," you reply.

Dad laughs. "Would you like to hold her? I'll let you if you're careful."

You glance from your father to the tarantula and back again.

"Sure," you say, trying to smile. But the smile is false, and the voice that replies isn't your own. It's the voice of fear.

"Hold out your hand," your father says. You do as you're told. Dad gently lifts Tarrie from his arm and places her on your hand.

(Turn to page 65)

Count Dracula slowly approaching a terrified young woman on the late show's nightmare movie.

"Come, my dear, I won't hurt you," the vampire says softly. He continues to advance slowly as she backs away from him. His grin reveals long, sharp fangs at the corners of his mouth.

"No, please, no," the woman says, retreating to the farthest corner of the room. Her hands are behind her back.

The count steps in front of her. His gaze focuses on her unprotected throat as he reaches for her. His upper lip curls away from his gums. As he pulls her toward him, she brings one hand from behind her back and thrusts it into his face. A tiny cross gleams above her fist.

The vampire hisses and takes a single step backward.

Then the lights go out in your house and the television blinks off.

You feel your way over to the coffee table in front of the sofa, then kneel and fumble for a candle and matches on the table.

Soon, flickering candlelight partially restores light to the room. As you rise, your shadow dances on the wall like a giant on the gallows.

You return to the front window. The streetlights are out, and the neighboring houses are dark, too. As frightening as it is, you're relieved: at least no one has cut the electric wires leading to your house in order to isolate you and Mitchie.

A bolt of lightning illuminates the sky momentarily. You see an overturned garbage can rolling across your front yard, spilling its contents onto the lawn as it rolls. Without pausing to think, you rush outside to gather up the trash and retrieve the garbage can before it rolls away into the street.

Stinging rain pelts your face and arms. The wind blows you off course several times as you rush toward the rolling garbage can. Finally, you manage to chase it down and spend two or three miserable minutes gathering up the garbage on the lawn and stuffing it back into the trash can. You carry the can back around to the side of the house where it will be protected from the wind.

After pausing briefly, you decide to go into the house via the back door because it's closer. You hurry around to the back porch, tug the screen door open, and turn the knob of the back door.

It's locked.

You don't really want to go back out into the rain again, so you decide to try to climb through Ralph's trap door. It will be a tight squeeze, but you think you can make it.

You're right: it *is* a tight fit. You manage to twist and wriggle your shoulders through the opening, but by the time your arms are free you wonder if you'll be able to work the rest of your body through the tiny door.

Then, just as you think you've made it, a bolt of lightning zigzags across the sky, filling the room with light.

From your face-down position on the floor, you have no trouble at all seeing the dirty black shoes and dark trousers of someone standing over you. Someone much larger than Mitchie and dressed too shabbily to be your father. Someone leering down at you in the darkness, enjoying your helplessness.

Someone who could only be

(Turn to page 67)

Mitchie's dead battery. The same one that was on the front porch earlier.

"Another of my hobbies," Uncle Frank says. "Restoring dead batteries."

By now you're convinced that Uncle Frank is crazy as a bedbug.

"Would you like to help me feed my bats?" Uncle Frank asks.

"If you don't mind, I think I'll go to bed," you say.

"Certainly," Uncle Frank says. "Would you like Jarvis to go with you?"

You shake your head no, eyeing the butler uneasily. He looms over you like a giant vulture.

You climb the steps and leave the cellar, glad to be away from your weird uncle.

As you pass the library, a movement inside the room catches your attention. You pause, unsure of what you saw and wondering whether you should investigate. Then the door begins to close slowly with loud metallic squeaks.

After another moment's hesitation, you open the door slowly and peek inside. As you do, your eyes widen in surprise. Across the room, a section of wall containing bookshelves is swiveling shut.

You rush over to the bookcase and halt its closing by inserting your foot in the opening. By tugging at the edge, you're able to expand the opening and peer into the darkness behind the door.

It's a hidden passageway!

A small gaslight on the wall partially illuminates the narrow passage. Although you cannot see anyone, it's obvious that someone used the passageway only seconds earlier. You wonder whether you should explore the passageway or go to bed.

Finally, curiosity gets the better of you. You step inside and permit the door to close behind you. As you glance around the dark room, you wonder who it was that preceded you into the passageway. It couldn't have been Uncle Frank or Jarvis; you left them downstairs in the cellar.

Whoever it was, you hope he isn't waiting for you somewhere along the narrow, foul-smelling passageway. There's nowhere to hide; the passageway is so narrow that you can almost touch the stone walls on either side of you The stones are as cold as death.

The passageway winds around to your left and then begins to rise. The air, you notice, is not only stuffy; it's also growing noticeably cooler as you go up.

After what seems like hours, but actually is no more than a minute, the floor levels off. You pause as the gaslight flickers on the wall. A draft of cold air sweeps across your shoulders, giving you a sudden chill.

You begin to walk again, more slowly than before. You round another curve and find a door in the wall similar to the one downstairs.

There's a small hole in the door at eye level. You walk over and peek through the eyehole.

The room you're looking into is too dark for you to see more than the outlines of vague shapes. Suddenly, though, a dim light appears in the room, and Uncle Frank's butler appears.

Jarvis is carrying a candlestick bearing a long, slender candle in one hand. Its flame arches backward and flickers uncertainly as he walks toward a canopied bed.

In his other hand, the butler is holding a thin, pointed instrument that looks like an ice pick.

Your gaze shifts to the bed. Mitchie is lying on the bed with the covers up to his chin. His eyes are open; he has a blank, drugged look on his face.

Mitchie doesn't seem to be afraid of Jarvis as he approaches the bed and stands over the boy, speaking quietly. Mitchie nods as if hypnotized.

Then, without warning, the butler leans forward and thrusts the ice pick toward Mitchie's face. As the boy opens his mouth to scream, you burst through the concealed doorway into the bedroom.

"No!" you shout. "You're not going to kill my brother!"

(Turn to page 69)

"Bo, get off me!" Mitchie cries, turning over and sitting up. The dog steps aside and licks Mitchie's face.

You call to Terry and Lisa, but there's no answer. "They're gone," you say.

"That's okay," Mitchie says, hugging the dog. "I'd rather have Bo, anyway."

Suddenly, a new sound reaches your ears. In the distance you hear a low, rumbling noise at the end of the road from which you came. In a matter of seconds, two headlights appear.

"It's a car, Mitchie! Get out of the road! Jump!"

And it *is* a car, hurtling toward you at high speed. You leap to one side as the car rushes past. It misses you by inches. As the car passes, you hear loud laughter inside the car.

You leap to your feet, enraged. "Come back!" you shout. "Come back, you bunch of sissies!"

Taillights blink on as the car grinds to a sudden stop. You hear car doors opening and drunken voices shouting "Let's get 'em!," and then feet pounding toward you on the dirt road. A flashlight beam pierces the fog.

"Into the woods, quick!" you whisper loudly to Mitchie. The two of you plunge into the thick underbrush. Several times you fall flat on your face, tripped up by roots and vines. Each time you leap to your feet and continue on blindly.

Giant spider webs block your path. You rush headlong through them, brushing them away. You hope an angry black widow spider isn't hitching a ride on the back of your neck.

"We've got to hide," you whisper to your brother. "Find the biggest bush you can and try to hide under it!"

"Okay." Mitchie isn't even panting, while you're huffing and puffing like an old-time locomotive.

The two of you duck into some heavy brush and wait, listening. All around you, the thrashing of the men hunting you is plainly evident. Off to your left in the woods, you can see a flashlight beam dancing in the trees.

Suddenly, a twig snaps near you, maybe four feet away. You hold your breath, not daring to trust your breathing. The way your heart is pounding like a jackhammer, the man *must* be able to hear it.

"Where are they?" a voice to your right calls out.

"I don't know," someone else replies loudly. "Joe, have you seen anything?"

"No," the man near you says in a deep voice. "Ain't nothing here but—"

He pauses and laughs softly. "Well, well, what have we got here?"

He's seen you!

Any second now, you expect a hand to grasp you roughly by the neck and jerk you out of the bush you're hiding in.

"Hey, guys," the man called Joe shouts. "Look at what I got here. It's

(Turn to page 71)

"Don't make a fist or close your fingers," Dad warns. "She might think you're trying to hurt her."

"Okay," you reply. Nothing on earth could get you to close your fingers now.

Tarrie almost covers your hand, she's so big. She's not as heavy as she looks, you realize; still, your fear makes you feel like you're holding a live hand grenade with the pin pulled.

You'd like to hold her up close to your face so you could study her more closely. But if you did that, she might leap from your hand onto your face and bite you before your father could pull her away.

So you hold her at nearly arm's length, until suddenly she begins to spider-walk slowly up your wrist and forearm. Your heart begins to race wildly.

"Uh, has she been fed yet?" you ask.

"I'll take her," Dad says, stepping up to you. "Don't make any sudden movements."

Keeping your eyes on the tarantula, you ask, "Does that include fainting?"

Dad laughs. With a surgeon's touch, he picks up Tarrie and replaces her in her cage. He latches and locks the cage as you wipe your perspiration-soaked hands on your shirt.

"I need to go back to the office for a minute," Dad says. He points to a door and tells you to go on into the next room and wait for him.

The room, you are aware, houses the alligators and crocodiles.

"Don't climb over the fence," Dad warns. "There are some dangerous characters in there."

"I won't," you say.

Something about your answer bothers your father, though.

"I'm serious," he says. "Stay out of the alligator pit. If one of them were to hit you with its tail—well, you'd never make it out alive!"

"Okay," you say, nodding.

Dad leaves through a door at the far end of the room. You turn and enter the room your father warned you about. After passing through the doorway, you hear the door click shut behind you.

You reach back and try to turn the doorknob. It won't budge. You're locked in.

If there's trouble, you're on your own—at least until Dad arrives.

(Turn to page 76)

your friend Terry Willis.

"What are you doing here?" you ask as you wriggle free and climb to your feet.

"I came in through the front door like any sane person," Terry replies. He smiles. "But never mind me, what about you? What have *you* been up to—a little midnight mud wrestling?"

You glance down at your soaked clothing and realize that you're going to have to mop the kitchen floor again. Then you lift your gaze back to Terry.

"What *are* you doing over here, anyway?"

Terry grins. "I got scared. I've always been afraid of lightning."

"Do your parents know you're here?"

"Did you think I woke 'em up and told 'em I was coming over here? Of *course* they don't know!" Terry leans over to wipe water off his raincoat onto the floor.

"Hey, you gotta get out of here," you say. "My folks will be home in a while, and you shouldn't be here when they get back."

"I guess you're right," Terry says. "Your mom doesn't exactly like me anymore."

"Well, it's your own fault," you argue. "Last time you had supper with us, you ate *nine* pieces of chicken."

"Hey, I'm a growing boy," Terry says.

You smile at your friend. "Mom says you're a growing nuisance."

"Well, if that's the way you feel about it, I'm leaving. I can take a hint." He turns and walks down the hall toward the living room.

"Are you going home?" you ask as Terry reaches the front door.

"Heck, no," Terry says, laughing. "I'm going over to Lisa's. It's only midnight."

Terry and Lisa are your best friends.

You lock the door behind Terry when he leaves. Then you go to your bedroom to put on dry clothes and return to the kitchen to mop the floor again. When you're finished, you return to the living room where Ralph is sleeping peacefully.

"You've been a great help tonight, Ralph," you say.

Ralph doesn't stir a muscle. If the convict broke in and kidnapped you and Mitchie, Ralph probably wouldn't bark until your dad was reading about it in the next morning's paper.

Suddenly, you hear a low, moaning sound coming from somewhere inside the house. It *could* be the wind, of course, or . . .

You decide to investigate. Gathering your courage and a candle from the coffee table, you walk cautiously back into the hallway.

The deep carpeting along the dark, narrow hallway muffles the sound of your footsteps. You notice with a sudden surge of fear how the silence inside the house contrasts with the howling wind outside.

Halfway down the hall, you pause. Something's wrong. You can feel it in your bones.

The moaning begins again as the noose dangles menacingly above your head.

(Turn to page 74)

Jarvis pauses and straightens, eyeing you with a surprised look on his face. The thermometer in his hand doesn't look so dangerous now that you're in the bedroom.

"I beg your pardon?" Jarvis asks.

"I—uh, I thought that, uh, you know, that, well . . . " Your voice sounds strange in your ears, as if it were coming from someone else.

"Really, this is most irregular," the butler says. "You thought I was going to *kill* your brother?"

Your gaze drops to the floor. "Well, you know . . . " Your voice fades away in embarrassment.

"No, I do *not* know," Jarvis replies. "Your brother indicated earlier that he was not feeling well. I was merely taking his temperature." He pauses, and then goes on. "And what, might I ask, were you doing in the passageway at this time of night?"

You shift your weight uneasily from one foot to the other. "I—I thought I saw someone going in there from the library downstairs, so I sort of tried to follow him, and—"

"You seem to have a very active imagination," Jarvis interrupts. "I'm afraid that Dr. Styne will find this news most distressing."

"Do you have to tell him?" you ask weakly.

Jarvis eyes you with a scowl. "Of course I shall. He should know that his young house guest has been wandering around at all hours of the night in rat-infested passageways."

"Rats? Oh, boy, I wanta see 'em!" Mitchie says.

"Shut up, Mitchie," you groan.

Jarvis turns to Mitchie and inserts the thermometer in the boy's mouth. Then, finding Mitchie's temperature to be normal, Jarvis leaves. He turns as he reaches the door.

"I trust that you'll remain in your room until morning?"

You nod dumbly.

"I have to go to the bathroom," Mitchie says.

The butler rolls his eyes heavenward, shakes his head, and closes the door behind him as he steps into the hall.

Mitchie climbs out of bed and follows Jarvis out of the room.

Ten minutes later, Mitchie still has not returned. You don't really notice his absence at first; you're too busy wondering who it was that entered the passageway before you.

After twenty minutes have passed and Mitchie still hasn't returned, you decide to look for him. You ease out of the room and slip quietly down the hall to the bathroom. Mitchie's not there. The room is empty.

They've taken Mitchie. And you think you know where he is. In the cellar.

(Turn to page 77)

a dog," Joe calls out. "And he don't look too friendly, either!" The man backs up slowly.

Bo growls fiercely as he steps toward the man.

"Nice doggie," the man says in a voice filled with sudden fear. Abruptly, he turns and dashes away with Bo in hot pursuit.

"Feet, don't fail me now!" the man shouts as he thrashes his way through the woods away from you. Then: "Ouch, he bit me on the— *Run! Run! It's a mad dog!*"

In the distance, car doors slam shut and an engine roars into life.

"Don't leave me! Wait for me, you dirty rats!" Joe shouts. But his voice is drowned out in the roar of the car accelerating away.

As you and Mitchie climb out of the bush, you wonder if Joe made it back to the car in time.

As if in answer to your question, Joe's voice rises like fog in the distance.

"I'll get you for this, you bums!" Joe shouts after his buddies. "Ow! Get away from me, you crazy dog!"

Then his voice fades away and disappears, too.

You turn to Mitchie. "I guess we'd better go through the woods." It's only a quarter of a mile to your house that way.

"Oh, boy," Mitchie says, "I love the woods!"

When, you wonder, is Mitchie going to grow up and start being afraid of dark places and scary things?

Dead Man's Woods are frightening even in the daytime. At night, and in the fog, the woods are terrifying beyond belief.

Somehow you make it through all right, though. Eventually you find yourself standing at the edge of the canal called Gator Creek. The canal separates Dead Man's Woods from the houses in your neighborhood.

You glance down at the slender pipe that spans the canal.

The pipe, only a few inches wide, is covered with slime. You'd rather not try to cross it, but your only other choice is to go back the way you came.

"I'll go first," Mitchie says. He darts across the 25-foot pipe. When he reaches the other side he turns and stands with his hands on his hips.

"Come on," he urges. "It's easy!"

Sure it is, you think. It's as easy as falling off a log!

You step out onto the pipe, trying not to look down at the lily pads and water below you. You walk slowly, sliding your feet along. Several times you overbalance and almost fall into the canal.

"You'd better not fall in," Mitchie warns helpfully. "They say there's alligators in the creek."

"Thanks, I needed that," you mumble, trying to concentrate on your feet and the pipe.

Suddenly, a thrashing sound in the water draws your attention. As you overbalance and start to topple forward into the creek, you see a pair of large unfriendly eyes and a dark shape moving toward you in the water.

Your last thought before you hit the water with a huge splash is that the dark shape gliding toward you in the water with upturned jaws is

(Turn to page 79)

You glance upward. Then, reaching up slowly, you take hold of the cord to the disappearing stairway leading to the attic.

The moaning continues.

And whatever is causing it is in the attic.

You pull down the stairs and unfold them to their full length. Gripping the candle in one hand, you climb the stairs one at a time. They creak and groan eerily beneath your weight.

The attic is piled high with boxes, trunks, and countless other items. You glance around, noting as you do so that the candle flame is flickering wildly. Wind must be coming in somewhere.

The attic window is open halfway. Curtains around the window are beating frantically, whipped by the shrieking wind.

In front of the curtains, a skeleton stands silently watching you.

Then, as if by signal, the skeleton rushes at you. Before you can move away, it is upon you, knocking you flat on your back.

The candle flickers out. As you look at the figure looming above you in the darkness, another burst of lightning illuminates the sky outside. You can see that the skeleton is headless.

(Turn to page 82)

The room is surprisingly dark. The only lighted area is enclosed by a low fence. Inside the fence, skylights overhead brighten a large, shallow cement pit.

You walk slowly toward the fence. Inside the pit, you see scores of alligators, crocodiles, and caimans with snouts like giant needle-nosed pliers. Everywhere—crawling over each other, snapping, hissing.

And behind you, from somewhere in the darkness near the wall, you hear the loud, hissing sound of something rushing toward you at incredible speed. Even as you turn, a kind of sixth sense warns you that it's

(Turn to page 80)

Before going downstairs, you quietly search each of the upstairs bedrooms. When you're finished, you've found no sign of Mitchie, Uncle Frank, or Jarvis.

You're more determined than ever now to search the basement.

You make your way to the staircase leading to the first floor and ease quietly down the broad spiral stairs.

As you reach the first floor landing, you hear voices approaching. You duck out of sight behind the ancient suit of armor and wait, listening.

It's Uncle Frank and Jarvis. They're talking as they approach.

"You're sure our young guest suspects nothing?" Uncle Frank asks.

"Oh, no, sir," Jarvis replies. "I believe my story about taking the boy's temperature was well received."

So he *wasn't* taking Mitchie's temperature after all!

"Let's hurry on," your uncle says. "We still have some preparations to make before the ceremony can begin."

They continue past your hiding place and head downstairs to the basement. When you hear the door click shut behind them, you move out of your hiding place. You tiptoe to the basement door and open it quietly.

You can hear voices talking as you close the door behind you. It's probably Uncle Frank listening to the television as he prepares Mitchie for whatever horrible fate he has in store for him.

You start down the stairs, recalling that the fourth step was the one that squeaked and gave you away earlier. This time, you pause on the third step and squat down to see what you can see.

Unfortunately, you can't see Mitchie, Uncle Frank, or Jarvis. They must be in the other, larger part of the room that's hidden from your view. To see that part of the room, you'll have to go all the way downstairs.

You can still hear the voices talking softly as you carefully step down beyond the fourth step onto the fifth step. As your weight shifts onto the lower stair, it emits a loud squeak.

Immediately, the talking stops. Seconds later, the lights go out, plunging the room into total darkness.

You turn to run back upstairs, when the door opens above you and Jarvis steps onto the landing. He is holding a candle in one hand and a large white box in his other hand.

"I believe your presence is desired downstairs," the butler says. The flickering candlelight shows a lifeless smile on his face.

"Mitchie!" you call out. "Are you down here, Mitchie?"

Around the corner of the room, you hear whispering. Finally, Mitchie replies.

"Yeah, c'mon down. Everything's okay."

Sure it is, you think. They've got Mitchie drugged or hypnotized so he'll say anything they want him to say. And they're just waiting for you so they can torture or kill both of you at one time!

"I think you'd better go," Jarvis says. "They're waiting for you below."

You're trapped. There's nowhere to run, nowhere to hide. You may as well get it over with.

Sighing heavily, you walk down the rest of the stairs and turn the corner.

(Turn to page 83)

the caretaker's watchdog, Bo. He swims past you, climbs out of the canal, and shakes himself vigorously.

You expect Mitchie to laugh his head off as you climb wetly out of the shallow creek. He's too interested in the dog, though, to do more than chuckle at your appearance.

What a night! you think as you and Mitchie walk away from the creek and toward the paved road that passes in front of your house. But at least it's almost over. You're within shouting distance of your house. Nothing can go wrong now!

Suddenly, a car rounds the corner with tires squealing. Its headlights are like giant laser beams splitting the foggy night.

The car grinds to a stop a few yards away from you. A dark figure climbs out of the car and glares at you angrily.

It's by far the most frightening sight you've seen all night.

(Turn to page 84)

only air from the ventilating fans.

And you're right. Relief flows over you like the air from the fans.

Your relief is short-lived, though. Even as you begin to relax, you are aware of a new sound in the room. It's a loud, hissing sound that could only belong to a very large alligator or crocodile. You hope the animal is *inside* the pit.

It's not, though.

It's a crocodile—a man-eater—at least eighteen feet long. And it's moving slowly toward you on the tile floor.

Even as you watch the great beast advance toward you, your horror is mingled with fascination. The crocodile's huge mouth is partly open in a permanent smile. You can see clearly the long rows of enormous teeth in its upper and lower jaws.

As the creature draws closer, you can even see the tears in its eyes. Legend has it that crocodiles cry before they kill their victims. You know that's not true, though. They "cry" to get rid of excess salt in their systems.

Knowing that doesn't help you to escape the great beast, however. You turn to run away, only to slip in a puddle of water near the fence. Your mind fills with terror as you feel yourself falling helplessly to the floor.

You try to scramble to your feet, but it's too late. The monster has you in its grasp, shaking you with twists of its head, shaking, shaking . . .

(Turn to page 85)

Of course it has no head.

It's not a skeleton. It's one of your mother's old dress forms she uses to make her own dresses. It's on rollers so she can move it easily from room to room.

You push the wire form away and climb to your feet. Then you hurry to the window and slam it shut.

Your heart is still pounding like jungle drums as you make your way to the stairs and start down.

In the dark, your foot misses the first step. You tumble forward, off-balance, and begin to tumble down, down, down.

It's as if you're falling in slow motion. You know that, if you don't land on your feet, you could easily receive a broken neck or a broken back when you hit the floor.

There's bad news and good news for you, though.

The bad news is that you don't land on your feet.

(Turn to page 86)

"Surprise!" a chorus of voices shouts as the lights come back on in the basement.

Standing before you is a smiling Uncle Frank. And Mitchie. And Mom and Dad. And even your best friends Terry and Lisa. All of them are smiling and laughing at the shocked expression on your face.

Above their heads is a large banner that reads, HAPPY BIRTHDAY!

"We really had you going, didn't we?" Uncle Frank says, stepping forward to put a friendly arm around your shoulders.

"Who, me?" you reply sheepishly. "No, you never fooled me for a second. I knew what was going on all the time."

You try to grin, but the smile never quite makes it all the way to the corners of your mouth.

The End

"I suppose you can explain all this," your father says in a no-nonsense tone of voice. He glances at his watch, then raises his eyes to stare at you.

"I suppose you have an explanation for being out wandering around, soaking wet, hours after you were supposed to have gone to bed."

"Not really," you reply in an unsteady voice.

Your father turns to Mitchie. "And what's your story, young man?"

"I was kidnapped!" Mitchie says quickly. "I didn't want to go. I—"

"Shut up, Mitchie," you mutter under your breath.

"No, go ahead," your father says. "I want to hear all about it. And when you're finished—"

He steps forward.

"Bo, no!" Mitchie calls out.

Bo, the night watchman's dog, growls once, then attacks. He thinks Mitchie is being threatened.

It is, you decide, the worst possible ending to the longest night of your life.

The End

only it's not a crocodile shaking you, it's your father. And you aren't in the Reptile House at the zoo; you're in your bed at home.

"Better get up now if you're going to the zoo with me today," Dad says.

You wipe the sleep away from your eyes. So it was a dream, after all. Just a bad dream.

"No, thanks, Dad," you reply. "I think I've had enough of spiders and snakes for a while."

The End

The good news is that you don't land on your neck or your back, either.

Instead, two things happen at once: the lights blink back on in the house and you find yourself being caught in the strong arms of your father. You stare up at him in surprise, relief, and embarrassment.

"Are you all right?" Dad asks as he sets you on your feet.

"Yes, sir," you say shakily.

"It's a good thing we came back when we did," he says.

"Yes, it is," your mother says, entering the hallway for the first time. Apparently, she didn't see your fall down the attic stairs.

"The kitchen is a mess," Mom continues. "It looks like a war went on in there. What happened while we were gone, anyway?"

"Nothing," you reply, shrugging. "I'll clean up the mess in the kitchen."

You turn and walk away, wondering who or what you'll find waiting for you in the kitchen. After all, it was neat as a pin last time you left the room.

The End

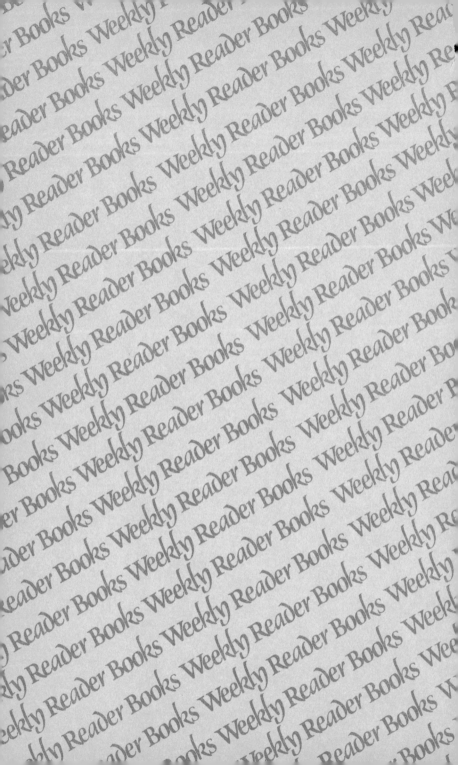